MOUNTAINT

EL DORADO COUNTY LIBRARY

J0589674

Rick took a deep breat...

He braced his back and started edging his way up. It was a tight fit. Rick's knees were almost in his mouth as he struggled through the chimney. Finally he topped out. "I'm up. There's a ledge here. I'll anchor and wait."

One at a time the other two boys emerged from the long crevice. There was barely enough room for all three to stand on the ledge. Above them was a granite overhang that jutted out almost six feet. Rick had already inserted one piton and was trying to find a toehold.

The overhang presented a dangerous problem. Rick, as the leader, had to find a way to go out and over the top. It would mean working upside down and trusting all his weight to the pitons he was able to hammer in along the way.

Spud and J.D. wrapped the rope around themselves and stood ready. Like an oversized spider, Rick climbed along the underside of the rock. He unclipped another piton from his belt and reached for his hammer.

Suddenly the carabiner, the aluminum oval snaplink attached to the piton, bent and Rick's body jerked and fell a few inches. Then with a sickening sound the carabiner popped open and the rope came completely loose.

Rick fell backward into space.

OTHER YEARLING BOOKS YOU WILL ENJOY:

JOURNEY, *Patricia MacLachlan*
SHILOH, *Phyllis Reynolds Naylor*
THE DISAPPEARING BIKE SHOP, *Elvira Woodruff*
THE SECRET FUNERAL OF SLIM JIM THE SNAKE,
Elvira Woodruff
AWFULLY SHORT FOR THE FOURTH GRADE,
Elvira Woodruff
THE SUMMER I SHRANK MY GRANDMOTHER,
Elvira Woodruff
HOW TO EAT FRIED WORMS, *Thomas Rockwell*
HOW TO FIGHT A GIRL, *Thomas Rockwell*
HOW TO GET FABULOUSLY RICH, *Thomas Rockwell*
BEETLES, LIGHTLY TOASTED, *Phyllis Reynolds Naylor*

YEARLING BOOKS/YOUNG YEARLINGS/YEARLING CLASSICS are designed especially to entertain and enlighten young people. Patricia Reilly Giff, consultant to this series, received her bachelor's degree from Marymount College and a master's degree in history from St. John's University. She holds a Professional Diploma in Reading and a Doctorate of Humane Letters from Hofstra University. She was a teacher and reading consultant for many years, and is the author of numerous books for young readers.

For a complete listing of all Yearling titles,
write to
Dell Readers Service,
P.O. Box 1045,
South Holland, IL 60473.

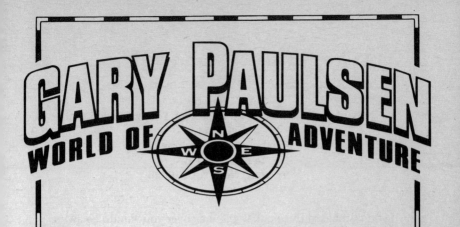

THE ROCK
JOCKEYS

EL DORADO COUNTY FREE LIBRARY
345 FAIR LANE
PLACERVILLE, CALIFORNIA 95667

A YEARLING BOOK

Published by
Bantam Doubleday Dell Books for Young Readers
a division of
Bantam Doubleday Dell Publishing Group, Inc.
1540 Broadway
New York, New York 10036

If you purchased this book without a cover you should be aware that this book is stolen property. It was reported as "unsold and destroyed" to the publisher and neither the author nor the publisher has received any payment for this "stripped book."

Copyright © 1995 by Gary Paulsen

All rights reserved. No part of this book may be reproduced or transmitted in any form or by any means, electronic or mechanical, including photocopying, recording, or by any information storage and retrieval system, without the written permission of the Publisher, except where permitted by law.

The trademarks Yearling® and Dell® are registered in the U.S. Patent and Trademark Office.

ISBN: 0-440-41026-6

Series design: Barbara Berger

Interior illustration by Michael David Biegel

Printed in the United States of America

April 1995

OPM   10   9   8   7   6   5   4   3   2

Dear Readers:

Real adventure is many things—it's danger and daring and sometimes even a struggle for life or death. From competing in the Iditarod dogsled race across Alaska to sailing the Pacific Ocean, I've experienced some of this adventure myself. I try to capture this spirit in my stories, and each time I sit down to write, that challenge is a bit of an adventure in itself.

You're all a part of this adventure as well. Over the years I've had the privilege of talking with many of you in schools, and this book is the result of hearing firsthand what you want to read about most—power-packed action and excitement.

You asked for it—so hang on tight while we jump into another thrilling story in my World of Adventure.

Gary Paulsen

THE ROCK
JOCKEYS

CHAPTER 1

Rick Williams ran his hand through his short brown hair and looked out the window. The sun wasn't up yet. He turned his attention back to what he was doing, rolled his sleeping bag tightly, and secured it to the frame of his metal packboard. He was the designated leader of this climb and he wanted no mistakes. Mentally he checked off his list of equipment: headlamp, mittens, sunglasses, food, extra clothing, canteen, cooking kit, compass . . .

The front door burst open. A sandy-haired boy who was about three inches taller than

Rick strode across the room and fell into the nearest chair. He grinned up at his friend. "I would have bet money on it. How many times have you inspected your pack this week?"

Rick turned red. "Come off it, J.D. You know the right equipment can mean the difference between life and death up there."

J.D. sat up. "There's not much chance of anybody getting hurt on good old Sugarloaf. Shoot, we've climbed that mountain a thousand times. It's baby stuff."

Rick looked at him. "You haven't talked to Spud yet, have you?"

"No, I—hey, what are you guys up to?" J.D. asked suspiciously.

"Did I hear someone mention my name?" A stocky boy with jet-black hair stepped into the room. He set his pack in the middle of the floor and pointed outside. "I left my climbing gear on the porch. We almost ready to go?"

J.D. stood up. "What did you forget to tell me this time, Spud?"

"Shhh." Rick held his hand up and looked back toward the stairs, where his parents'

bedroom was. "We don't want everybody to know."

"This spring break we're doing things a little different, J.D.," Spud whispered. "The Rock Jockeys are finally going on a *real* climb. We've worked hard to get in shape and practiced our heads off. Now it's time to put it all to the test."

"Where are we going? Elk Mountain? Timmons Peak?"

Spud grew serious. "We're going up the north face—Devil's Wall."

J.D. sucked in a breath. Devil's Wall was the most dangerous mountain face in the area. "Does your dad know we're not going to Sugarloaf?" he asked.

Rick shook his head. "No, but it's all right. Dad's our teacher and he knows we're good. He's responsible for everything we know about rock climbing. He'll be proud when we become the first climbers in history to make it up the north face."

"After he kills us." J.D. ran his hand through his hair. "I don't know . . . I didn't really come prepared for a climb like this."

"Got it covered." Spud raced to the porch and came back with extra food and supplies. He motioned for J.D. to put the stuff in his own pack.

J.D. was still worried. "Maybe we should wait till summer. The top is probably covered with ice and snow now."

"Come on, J.D." Rick picked up his pack. "So far everybody in town makes fun of the Rock Jockeys. This is our big chance to show them we're serious climbers. Think how famous we'll be: the first, not to mention the youngest, climbers to make it all the way up Devil's Wall." Rick paused. "And there's also the bomber to think of."

"Don't tell me you guys believe that stupid rumor?"

The whole town knew the story about how a World War II bomber had supposedly crashed somewhere on the top of Devil's Wall. The latest gossip was that the crew had all been killed and the government hadn't been able to recover the plane.

"What if it's true?" Spud asked. "What if a

bomber actually crashed up there? Wouldn't it be neat to get to see it up close?"

"No way." J.D. shook his head. "The government has had every kind of helicopter and search team up there you can name. They've gone over every inch of that mountain from the air and they haven't found a thing."

Spud slapped J.D. on the back. "That's because they didn't have the Rock Jockeys helping them."

CHAPTER 2

 J.D. looked down at the gentle, tree-studded ridge behind them. It had been simple enough. They really hadn't had to use any special skills to climb it. It had been more of a hike than anything.

He turned back to the sheer rock face in front of them. Devil's Wall was straight up and down. From where they were standing they couldn't see the snow-covered top. By Spud's calculations, it would take a full day to make it up there . . . barring accidents.

J.D. shook his head. "Rick, your dad always

taught us to leave word with someone about where we're going. I'm not sure this is such a good idea."

Spud tied the rope in a bowline knot and checked to make sure he had the equipment he needed on his belt. "We left word with Toby Wilson. If we're not back in four days, he's supposed to get help."

"Lead man ready," Rick yelled from next to the wall.

Spud cupped his hand. "Belayer ready." He looked at J.D. "Well?"

J.D. hesitated, then grabbed the rope and tied off. "End man ready."

The first thirty feet was slow going. Rick picked his way carefully, driving metal pitons into the rock face with his hammer, then pulling himself up. Every ten feet he had to stop and let Spud work his way up behind him. Spud in turn waited for J.D. to bring up the rear.

The rock face was black and shiny with silver-lined cracks that glistened in the sun. It was an almost completely flat wall of smooth rock, offering them no easy way up. Cautiously Rick led them higher, hammering and pulling until the muscles in his arms ached. Finally he stopped to catch his breath.

"Resting," Rick called down. "Chimney ahead."

J.D. and Spud were hanging below him. They both knew that a chimney meant hard work. It was a large crevice in the rock. In order to get up it, you had to use your back on one side and your feet on the other, inching up inside, hoping nothing got jammed.

Spud reached in his pocket for a handful of trail mix. "How are you doing down there?"

J.D. waved up at him. "So far so good. What's taking you slowpokes so long?"

"I heard that." Rick looked down at him. "I'd drop something on your thick head, but then I'd just have to carry your carcass back down and it isn't worth it."

"You just make sure *you* don't fall on my thick head."

Rick took a deep breath. "Climber ready."

He braced his back and started edging his

way up. It was a tight fit. Rick's knees were almost in his mouth as he struggled through the chimney. Finally he topped out. "I'm up. There's a ledge here. I'll anchor and wait."

One at a time the other two boys emerged from the long crevice. There was barely enough room for all three to stand on the ledge. Above them was a granite overhang that jutted out almost six feet. Rick had already inserted one piton and was trying to find a toehold.

The overhang presented a dangerous problem. Rick, as the leader, had to find a way to go out and over the top. It would mean working upside down and trusting all his weight to the pitons he was able to hammer in along the way.

Spud and J.D. wrapped the rope around themselves and stood ready. Like an oversized spider, Rick climbed along the underside of the rock. He unclipped another piton from his belt and reached for his hammer.

Suddenly the carabiner, the aluminum oval snaplink attached to the piton, bent and

Rick's body jerked and fell a few inches. Then with a sickening sound the carabiner popped open and the rope came completely loose.

Rick fell backward into space.

Spud and J.D. held their ground. Using a hip belay, Spud gave a little slack when Rick hit the end of the rope. The weight of Rick's body pulled Spud and slammed him against the rock face. But he held on for all he was worth. J.D. anchored around a rock and dug his feet in.

"We've got you, Rick . . . Rick?" Spud anxiously tried to get a look over the side.

First there was silence. Then a weak voice called up, "I'm a little shook up, but all right. Pull anytime you're ready."

J.D. and Spud strained on the rope trying to get him back to the ledge. Rick helped every time he got a chance, using tiny cracks and footholds.

When they hauled him over the edge, his face was white and covered with sweat. He rested for a few minutes and then shakily got to his feet.

"Hold on." Spud steadied him. "You should take it easy for a while."

Rick shook his head. "No time. If we're going to make it to the top before dark we have to hustle."

J.D. readjusted his pack. "It would be better to spend the night out here on the face than to have the coroner scrape us up off the bottom."

Spud swallowed. "If you want to switch places, Rick, I'll take lead for a while."

Rick set his jaw. "I'm the designated leader on this climb." He turned to the overhang. "And I'll see it through to the end. Now let's get going."

CHAPTER 3

"Don't you look pretty?" Rick frowned as he hauled J.D. on top of the overhang.

J.D. touched his cheek. Blood came off on his hand. "I guess I must have scraped it coming over."

The three of them sat on the narrow overhang, resting and looking down at what they had accomplished so far. They were halfway up the wall with no major problems. But this was nothing; other climbers had made it this far. What had stopped them was what still lay ahead.

The rock wall above them was as smooth as polished black marble. There were no crevices and no ledges. They would have to fight for every inch.

Rick looked at his friends. J.D. and Spud nodded silently. Rick stood up and started. His job would be to make the trail. Their job was to make sure he lived through it.

The sun was already on its way down. The climb was taking longer than any of them had expected. But Rick was determined. He kept going, working at a snail's pace hammering and moving up.

The other two followed, always keeping a watchful eye. At the slightest hint of a slip, Spud and J.D. pulled the rope taut and prayed the pitons would hold them.

Rick was fast becoming exhausted. The climb had taken a lot out of him. He looked down. Spud and J.D. resembled tiny insects trailing along behind him. Everything looked so small and insignificant from up here.

"Putting on headlamp," Rick yelled down. He reached in his pack and pulled it out.

They were losing the light. From here to the top they would have to work wearing the lamps.

The headlamp threw weird shadows and made it hard to decide where to hammer. Rick unclipped a piton and started to pound it in. The rock was rotten and small pieces came loose in his hand. A big chunk fell out. He grabbed for it and missed.

"Rock!"

Spud covered his head and buried his face in the wall as the rock sailed by. J.D. wasn't as lucky. The chunk smashed into his shoulder.

"You rock brain. What are you trying to do up there—kill me?"

Rick breathed a sigh of relief. He knew if J.D. was yelling at him, he wasn't hurt too bad. He shouted back, "Just trying to keep you guys on your toes."

"Wait till we reach the top," J.D. called. "I'll show you how much I appreciate it."

They worked in silence for the next two hours. The only sounds in the still evening were the clang of the hammer and the groans of the three climbers.

Rick felt above him for the next place to hammer. There was none. Instead his hand grabbed a flat rock. Using both arms, he hoisted himself over the edge. He sat on his knees and pointed his headlamp in front of him. There were patches of snow and trees everywhere.

A slow grin started in one corner of his mouth. He threw his arms in the air triumphantly.

"We made it!"

CHAPTER 4

 They hadn't stopped grinning and high-fiving each other since J.D. had finally pulled himself over the top. No one in history had ever climbed the entire face of Devil's Wall and lived to tell about it.

Setting up camp for the night had taken less time than usual. The boys were too happy to realize how exhausted they were.

When the sun came up, J.D. ignored it. He turned over inside his sleeping bag and tried to get comfortable. He was almost sound asleep again when he heard the other two tramp back into camp.

Spud winked at Rick. "I heard its favorite meal was human flesh wrapped in a bedroll."

Rick shook his head. "No, it spits out the sleeping bag and bites the victim's head off, letting the blood slowly drain into its hideous mouth."

J.D. sat up. "What are you two morons talking about? Can't you see I'm trying to sleep here?"

"Rick thought he heard something moving around in those trees last night." Spud looked at Rick. "Should I tell him what we suspect?"

Rick tried to keep a straight face. "He might as well know what we're up against."

"We think it's . . . the Abominable Snowman."

J.D. lay back down. "You guys are hilarious. I'm going back to sleep."

"Come on, J.D." Spud pulled on the end of the sleeping bag. "How can you sleep with that bomber somewhere up here?"

"I told you, it's not here." J.D. rolled over. "Otherwise the government would have found it by now." He was quiet for a moment, then quickly turned back to his friends. "You didn't really hear anything out there, did you, Rick?"

"No, we were just kidding about that. But it's really dark and desolate up here. There's something about this place that gives me the creeps."

"I'm not worried. In the first place, there's no way anything could get up here," J.D. said. *"We* barely made it. I doubt if there are even any animals up here."

"He's got a point there," Spud said. "Unless maybe they were airlifted here."

Rick thought about it. "Mountain goats. I bet there are mountain goats up here . . . and birds. There are probably all kinds of birds."

Spud pushed the coals in the campfire around with a stick. "I just hope nothing decides to come visit us in the middle of the night."

J.D. stood up and stretched. "Like I said, I'm

not worried. One sniff of you and it'll run the other way." He pulled his boots on and slipped into his jacket. "Well, what are you bums waiting for? Let's go do some exploring."

CHAPTER 5

 Rick stopped to check his compass. "I didn't know the top of Devil's Wall had so many trees. Sure would be easy to get lost up here."

J.D. looked up. The trees were so thick he could hardly see the sky. "It's like that old saying about not being able to see the forest for the trees. I bet it would be something to look at if we weren't right in the middle of it."

Spud checked the lens on his camera. He looked up suddenly. "Did you guys see that?"

Rick elbowed him. "Looks like your own ghost stories are starting to get to you."

"No really. It was over in that direction." Spud pointed to a dark stand of trees. "I thought I saw something sparkle."

"I didn't see anything," Rick said. "But I'm not having any luck in this direction. We can take a look if you want."

Spud led the way into what seemed like a black hole. The trees were so dense they blocked out the sun. Branches and pine needles were scattered on the ground, but nothing else. He shrugged his shoulders. "I must have been seeing things."

"Wait." Rick grabbed his arm. "There's something shiny over there."

The boys ran through the brush in front of them and moved back some branches.

"Would you look at that!" Spud's eyes widened.

"What is it?" J.D. moved closer to the dome-shaped object.

"A ball turret." Spud knelt to get a better look. "I read about these. It was the gunner's station on the bottom of the B-17. The ball gunner actually had to get in this thing to shoot at the enemy. It must have broken off

21

somehow." He looked through an opening. "Can't tell much about it. It's pretty well smashed."

Rick looked around. "Do you know what this means?"

Spud nodded. "If the turret is here, the rest of the plane can't be far away. Come on."

The boys spread out, working their way through the thick underbrush.

"Over here!" Spud waved at them frantically. Rick and J.D. came running.

Propped against some trees in front of Spud was a giant piece of a wing that had been sheared off from the body of the plane.

They stepped around the wing, moving forward quickly. And there it was.

The body of the B-17.

It had a gash the size of a car on one side and the tail section was in fragments. Pieces of engines and propeller lay scattered everywhere.

They stood transfixed, in awe of the giant plane. It had painted lettering on the side that read DEATH ANGEL.

Finally Rick broke the spell. "Let's get some

pictures and see if we can tell anything about the crash."

Spud started clicking his camera. They took turns posing beside the plane.

J.D. stuck his head through the opening in the side. "I wonder if we could take a look inside?"

"I don't see why not." Rick ran his hand along the plane. "She looks pretty stable."

J.D. crawled through the gash, walked in darkness down the body, and opened the door to the cockpit. He stopped, swallowed hard, and hurried back to the opening.

"What's the matter?" Rick asked. "You look kinda sick."

"I'll be all right in a second." J.D. turned away. "You guys go on in."

Rick and Spud moved to the hole and stepped through. The old fifty-caliber machine guns were still in place. In the corner of the plane near the guns was the radio. The two boys looked into the open door of the cockpit.

Old bloodstains covered the seats.

Spud made a face. "Kinda gross, isn't it?"

"Strange is more like it."

"What do you mean?"

Rick scratched his head. "If we're the first ones to find the bomber . . . then where's the crew?"

J.D. stuck his head back in. "I was just thinking about that. The government must have beat us to it after all."

"You'd have thought we would have heard something about it. Oh well, take some pictures anyway, Spud. It's part of the reason we came."

As Spud focused his camera, Rick moved down to the nose of the plane. The navigator's station was in shambles and the nose cone was shattered. He turned to leave and bumped into a solemn-looking J.D.

"I didn't think finding it would be like this, Rick."

Rick nodded. "Let's get out of here. There's no use for us to hang around. I've seen enough for now anyway."

CHAPTER 6

They walked back to camp in silence. Spud had stuffed everything he could carry in his pack —machine-gun shells, the radio receiver, even a piece of a prop. What he had really wanted was a flight jacket, but he hadn't been able to find one.

Spud sat his heavy pack on the ground. "I'm beat. I guess yesterday's climb took more out of me than I thought."

J.D. stirred up the coals from the morning's fire and started lunch. "I was just thinking . . . this mountaintop can't be all that big."

"It isn't." Rick helped him set up the grill.

"Maybe a few square miles at the most. Why?"

J.D. rubbed his chin. "Since we have until Thursday to get back, why don't we do some more exploring?"

"You must be awfully fond of trees," Spud said. "Besides the plane, there's nothing else up here to see."

Rick opened a can of peaches. "There's no reason why we can't. Spud's right though. There doesn't seem to be much here except trees."

J.D. looked puzzled. "That's the part that's throwing me. The trees up here are so close together, how did the government get the bodies out?"

Rick shrugged. "They've got some pretty specialized equipment nowadays."

J.D. spooned some beans into his mouth. "All these years, since we were kids—heck, since our dads were kids—there have been rumors about a plane crashing on Devil's Wall. We know they launched a full-scale search a few years ago. If they found it, why didn't we see anything in the papers about it?"

"Maybe the plane was on some secret mission. You know how the government is." Spud gulped down the rest of the peaches and pointed at J.D.'s plate. "You gonna eat the rest of those beans?"

J.D. shook his head and handed him the plate. "Here." He stood up and looked into the forest. "You guys are probably right, but since we're here I'd like to take another look around."

Spud laughed and made a spooky noise. "Who do think got the crew? The boogeyman?"

"Cut it out, Spud." Rick threw a pebble at him. "We might as well take a look after lunch. It couldn't hurt. And then, when we get back down, we can say we know everything there is to know about this mountain."

CHAPTER 7

"Hey, wait up. My pack is heavier than yours." Spud tried to move his pack around to adjust the bulky weight. "And another thing, why are we bringing all our stuff with us?"

Rick led the way up the ridge. He stopped to let Spud catch up. "It's not our fault you tried to stuff the whole plane in your pack. And if you had been listening, you'd know we decided to bring our gear and make camp when it got dark. That way we wouldn't have to go back each night and waste time."

"Why didn't you just leave the heavy stuff back there?" J.D. asked. "It's not like there's anybody up here to steal it."

"I'm not taking any chances." Spud started walking. "Someday this stuff is going to be worth a lot. Then you guys will be sorry you gave me a hard time about it."

So far they hadn't really discovered anything new. The mountain had a few ridges and narrow valleys, but they were all covered with trees like the place where they had found the bomber.

J.D. topped a ridge and leaned against a tree. He started to sit down. "Do you guys hear that?"

Rick came up behind him. "I can't hear anything over Spud's huffing and puffing."

J.D. scanned the valley below looking for an open spot. "I'm not sure, but it sounds like there's water down there."

They made their way down the other side of the ridge and at the bottom they found a clear mountain stream running full with pure, cold water.

Spud sat his pack down and scooped handfuls of water into his mouth. "This is great. It beats that bottled stuff any day."

J.D. walked upstream and filled his canteen. It was beautiful here. He wondered how many people besides them had ever had the privilege of getting to see this spot. To his left he noticed what looked like a natural path to another part of the forest. It was overgrown with plants and bushes but it looked easier to follow than what they had been through so far. "When you guys are ready, let's go this way." J.D. pointed. "Maybe Spud won't have to work so hard."

Spud wiped water off his face with his sleeve. "Why don't we just camp here?"

Rick picked up Spud's pack. "Here, I'll swap you for a while." He swung the heavy pack around to his back. "You be careful with mine, though. We could have a little trouble getting back down if you lose it."

"Thanks, Rick. I'll do you a favor someday." Spud carelessly slung Rick's pack over one shoulder and started up the hill.

J.D. was already halfway up the next ridge.

The natural trail was perfect to follow. They didn't have to fight their way through the brush or go around any difficult areas.

Spud trotted up beside J.D. "Now I see why you guys were moving so fast. This is nothing compared to what I was carrying." He moved ahead while J.D. waited for Rick.

Just as J.D. turned to look back, he heard a loud screech.

Spud was gone.

CHAPTER 8

 Rick and J.D. dropped their gear and ran to the spot where Spud had vanished. A deep hole was in the middle of the path. Leaves and branches had covered the opening and Spud had stepped right into it.

"Spud!" Rick called. "Are you okay?"

They heard a low moan down in the hole. J.D. ran back to his pack for his headlamp and pointed it down into the pit. "I see him. Looks like he's almost at the bottom."

"Spud, can you hear us?" Rick called again.

"I hear you."

"Good. Hang on, I'm going to throw you a rope."

Another moan came from the hole. "I think I busted my arm, Rick. It hurts bad."

J.D. yelled down the hole, "Try not to move, we'll come down after you." He took off his climbing rope and unwound it.

Rick grabbed the end and tied it around himself. "Use that tree to help lower me. When I get down there, I'll put the rope on Spud."

J.D. didn't argue. He handed Rick his headlamp and moved around the tree to wait for Rick's signal.

"Lower when ready."

J.D. let the rope out slowly.

"Give me some slack. I'm almost there, but it's getting real tight in here. There's not much room to work."

Rick pressed his back and feet against both sides of the narrow hole and slipped the rope up over his head. Then he lowered it to Spud. "I'm as close as I can get. Put your head and arms through the loop and J.D. will pull you up to me."

Rick heard Spud groan in agony as he lifted his broken arm through the rope. "I'm in. Pull when ready."

J.D. pulled. Nothing happened. Spud was wedged in tight. "It's no use," Spud yelled up. "I'm stuck."

"Tie off and lower a pick down here," Rick shouted to J.D. "I'm going to try to dig him out."

J.D. made sure the rope was tight and went to his pack for a climbing pick. He lowered it using a ball of twine. "Heads up down there. Here it comes."

"This is going to be tricky, Spud." Rick edged his way around until he was upside down. Still using his back and feet to keep from falling, he inched farther down the hole.

When he got closer he could see that Spud was in a tight little ball. His knees were under his chin and his left arm hung limply to the side. Carefully, Rick started digging around his friend until Spud's legs could move a little.

Rick cupped his hand. "Try it again, J.D."

J.D. pulled and this time Spud moved up a few inches.

"Hold on," Rick yelled. "Let me get out of his way."

Rick worked his way up a few feet and tried to get as far to one side as he could. "Okay, J.D. . . . pull!"

In a few seconds, Spud was beside Rick. His face was pale and he was obviously in pain. Rick helped push him up. J.D. kept pulling until he dragged Spud out over the edge.

J.D. quickly slipped the rope over Spud's shoulders. "You all right?"

"I've been better."

J.D. helped him to a tree and propped him against it. "Can you hold on here till I get Rick out?"

Spud closed his eyes. "Don't worry about me. I'll be fine."

"Dropping rope," J.D. yelled. He released the end with the loop down into the hole. "Can you reach your backpack, Rick?"

Rick had been working on that problem. He could see his pack at the bottom of the hole, but it was so narrow he didn't see how he could get to it.

He slid into the loop and yelled up to J.D., his voice echoing in the hole. "The only way to get it is to go in headfirst. Even then it'll be a tight squeeze."

J.D. looked anxiously down the hole. "I don't like it, Rick. Let the stuff go. We'll make do without it."

"No way. I'm already here. I might as well make a try for it. Get ready."

Rick wrapped the rope around one leg and started down. "Keep giving me slack."

The hole was only a foot wide at the bottom. Rick could see the pack but couldn't quite reach it. "Pull me up about two feet. I've got some digging to do."

He dug at the sides of the hole until his shoulders would fit through. "Okay, give me slack."

Rick pointed the light down the hole. There was something else at the bottom beside the backpack. It looked like a log or rocks. He worked his way down and reached as far as he could. The tips of his fingers found the strap on the pack.

He put the pick in his belt and hauled the pack up. There wasn't much room to see with the pack in his way, but he pointed the light anyway. His eyes widened in disbelief.

The things at the bottom of the hole were bones.

Human bones and a skull.

Chapter 9

Rick turned his head and clutched the pack tightly. "I've got it, J.D. Get me out of here."

J.D. used the pine tree for leverage and pulled Rick up.

Rick threw the pack over the top edge of the hole and crawled out behind it. "How's Spud?" He took the rope and headlamp off.

"I'm fine," Spud answered, "except I feel like a total jerk."

Rick brought the first-aid kit from his pack. "I wouldn't if I were you. Turns out you weren't the first guy to fall in that hole."

"What are you talking about?" Spud tried to sit up and winced with pain.

"Easy. Lie back down so we can splint that arm." Rick gently felt Spud's arm until he located the break just below the elbow. J.D. found two straight sticks for splints, and together they wrapped it with elastic bandage from the kit.

"Sorry we don't have any painkiller. You'll just have to tough it out." Rick put the kit back in his pack. "Can you stand?"

"In a minute. What's this about me not being the first one to fall in that hole?"

"You're not going to believe this. When I was reaching for my pack I nearly came up with some bones and a skull."

"Human?" J.D. suddenly looked sick.

Rick nodded. "Sorry, guys, but we're not the first ones to explore up here."

"I don't care. I'm just glad I didn't wind up like the last guy." Spud tried to get to his feet.

J.D. helped him stand. "It's gonna be dark soon. We better find a place to camp."

Rick shouldered both his pack and Spud's. "Hopefully there'll be a good spot just over this ridge. If not, I'm leaving some of this stuff for the next fortune hunters." He looked back at Spud. "It's amazing what some people will do to get out of work."

CHAPTER 10

Spud's eyes flew open. For a moment he thought he had dreamed the whole thing. Then the pain in his arm reminded him that it was definitely real.

His arm was killing him and, except for the last couple of hours, he hadn't really slept at all. Spud raised himself on his good elbow and looked around the campsite. He was alone.

They had left him some cooked powdered eggs and tea near the fire. He made his way to it and awkwardly sat down to eat.

"How's your arm this morning, Sleeping

Beauty?" Rick moved a large tree branch and stepped into camp.

"It's a little swollen and it aches—kind of like a toothache. But other than that, it's coming around. Where's J.D.?"

"Out looking for the best route back through the woods so we can get you off this mountain quicker."

"You guys don't worry about me. My right arm is just as good as ever." Spud flexed his muscle and rotated his right arm in a circle. "I'm a mountain-climbing machine."

J.D. stepped out of the trees. "We weren't worried about you. We're just getting kinda tired of this place." He looked at Rick. "It's brushy all the way. I say we travel as the crow flies. It'll be hard no matter which way we take, but that will be the shortest route."

Rick checked Spud's arm and loosened the bandage in a couple of places. "I'll kill the fire. You guys make sure we have everything."

When they were ready to leave, J.D. picked up Spud's heavy pack. Spud put his hand out to stop him. "I don't need all that stuff. Let's lighten it and then I can carry it."

"Are you sure?"

Spud nodded and started pulling things out. He took out the prop and a little black book fell on the ground. Rick reached down and picked it up. "What's this?"

Spud shrugged. "I haven't had a chance to look at it. It's probably a logbook or something. I found it wrapped in a plastic sack stuffed down in a hole in the wall of the plane."

Rick opened it and started reading. He flipped through a few pages. "It's a diary." Rick sat down on a nearby boulder. "This is incredible."

"What?" The other two boys crowded around him.

"One of those guys survived the crash. Listen to this. . . ."

August 25, 1945

It is now the third day since the crash. I have decided to keep this journal as a

way of passing the time until help arrives.

My name is Lieutenant James Dowling. I am—was—the navigator of the ship Death Angel *and am the only surviving member of the crew. Miraculously I have come through with only a flesh wound to my forehead.*

Rick turned the page and continued.

I have explored my surroundings and have found them hostile. There is no immediate food source and as yet I have not been able to find water.

August 28, 1945

Today I buried the crew. It was hard work in such rocky ground, but it needed doing. I have been using the plane for shelter and it is adequate although it is growing colder each day. But that is not my main concern. If help does not come soon I will surely starve to death.

The following page was blank except for one word.

Food.

The next entry wasn't dated.

I have found water and it has given me a little hope but on my second trip to the stream I nearly fell into what looks like a bottomless pit.

"He must be talking about the same hole I fell in." Spud looked over Rick's shoulder. "Does he say how those bones got in there?"

Rick flipped though the pages. "It's hard to tell. From here on he sort of rambles."

Dan Thorton was a great pilot. He made it through the entire war without a scratch. We were on our last flight together. It was Dan's idea to stop off at the club for a couple of farewell drinks.

We had great plans for civilian life. Dan was going into business for himself. He invited us all to come in with him and

run a small airfield near his home in Memphis.

The next paragraph was smeared. Rick could barely make it out.

I set the course and then relaxed. The next thing I knew the captain was on the radio. Something had gone wrong with the plane. It was going down and he didn't have a clue where we were. I tried desperately to get us back on course, but by that time it was too late. Too late.

My fault, all of it. As navigator I am responsible.

J.D. let out a low whistle. "Poor guy," he said. "Up here starving to death with all that guilt on his shoulders. Does he say anything else?"

"There's one more entry. It's dated much later, in September. That's odd. . . ." Rick scanned it quickly.

"Well?" Spud asked. "What does it say?"

Rick snapped the book shut. "Nothing." He moved to the spot where they had built the fire earlier, kicked some of the dirt off the coals, and threw the little book on it.

Spud watched the flames lick at the yellowed pages. Within seconds the book had turned to ash. "Why'd you do that? That's a historical document."

"Not anymore." Rick picked up his gear and headed down the hill.

"I don't get it." Spud scratched his head. "What's wrong with him?"

J.D. frowned. "I'm not sure. But I'm starting to piece it together."

"Are you gonna let me in on it?"

"You remember earlier when we found the plane and we were wondering why the government didn't tell anybody anything about the crash or finding the bodies?"

"Yeah? So?"

"I think they put it together too when they found the lieutenant's body in the plane and didn't find all of the crew in their graves."

"What are you talking about?"

"You remember those bones we found in the bottom of that hole?"

Spud nodded.

"How do you think the lieutenant managed to stay alive as long as he did?"

Spud shrugged. "I don't know. Maybe he—wait a minute. You're not saying . . . I mean, you don't think he dug up one of those guys for food, do you?"

J.D. picked up the rest of the gear. "We may never know. The bones are at the bottom of a pit and Rick just burned the only other evidence."

CHAPTER 11

 "Here, let me carry that." J.D. reached for Spud's gear.

Spud moved it out of J.D.'s reach. "I can manage. Besides, I'll be packing it off the mountain tomorrow so I better get used to it."

Rick hadn't said a word since burning the diary. He stopped and turned. "You don't have to come down with us tomorrow."

"What are you talking about? Sure I do."

Rick chose his words carefully. "If J.D. and I leave you our rations, you could stay up here until we get down. As soon as we hit bottom we'll go for help and—"

"Forget it. I'm a Rock Jockey. There's no way I'm going back in a helicopter." Spud stiffened and headed down the hill in front of them.

"I didn't mean to make him mad. I was just trying to make it easier on him." Rick sighed. "If anything happened to Spud on the way down, I'd never forgive myself."

J.D. cocked his head. "Tell me the truth. If you were in his shoes, would you go back in a chopper?"

Rick looked sheepish. "I see what you mean."

J.D. laughed. "We better catch up with him before he gets to the north face and starts down without us."

They half ran through the brush until they found Spud. He glared back at them and kept walking.

J.D. winked at Rick. "You know, I was just thinking. Tomorrow would be a good time for us to try that new impaired-climber move I was reading about."

"You mean the one where we wrap the injured man in a sleeping bag and drop him in a free fall to the bottom?"

"That's the one."

Spud turned. "If you airheads think I'm gonna let you—"

Rick and J.D. started laughing. "Got ya!"

CHAPTER 12

 The sun was just coming up. Rick took a sip of his tea and threw a stick on the fire. "Before we start off the mountain, I guess I owe you guys an explanation about the lieutenant's diary."

"Diary?" Spud looked at J.D. "What diary? I don't know anything about any diary. Do you?"

J.D. shook his head. "Never saw one."

Rick half smiled. Then his look grew serious again. "I was thinking of the lieutenant's family. I figure the government's already made its report and after all these years his family doesn't need this kind of shock. The lieutenant did what he had to in order to survive. Any of us might have done the same in his position."

"Nobody here is arguing with you, Rick." J.D. was equally serious. "Spud and I talked it over last night. Your dad taught us not to judge someone unless you've walked a mile in their shoes. And I sure wouldn't have wanted to be in Lieutenant Dowling's shoes when the bomber crashed."

"So we're all agreed," Spud said. "The only thing we found up here was an empty, wrecked bomber." He had taken the bandage off his arm and was trying to rewrap it.

Rick watched his progress. One of the sticks fell on the ground. The other one was turned sideways. Rick folded his arms. "I know you're a Rock Jockey and everything, but do you want some help?"

"Shut up and get over here." Spud held the elastic bandage out to him.

J.D. looked on as Rick wrapped the arm. "You guys realize that we're gonna be famous when we get back?"

Rick glanced up. "I've been giving that some thought." He tied off the bandage and started collecting his gear. "Maybe we could use our skills to help out around here."

J.D. put out the fire. "What are you talking about?"

"Well, there are a lot of dangerous mountain ranges nearby." Rick uncoiled his rope. "And people like Lieutenant Dowling are always getting lost or stuck on them somewhere. Then the authorities have to go out and locate rescue teams. . . ."

"And you think they should call us?" Spud heaved his pack onto his back and checked his rope.

"Why not?" Rick moved to the edge of the cliff and grinned. "We're the best, aren't we?" He reached down and hooked his rope to the first carabiner. "Lead man ready."

Spud put his thumb in the air. "Belayer ready."

J.D. waved. "End man ready."

Rick dropped over the side. "Last one down buys the other two pizza."

"Do you think he's serious?" Spud looked back at J.D.

"About what? The pizza or us becoming a rescue team?"

Spud laughed. "Both."

"He better not be serious about the pizza because I'm the end man. About helping people, why not?" J.D. smiled. "After all—we're the Rock Jockeys."

GARY PAULSEN
ADVENTURE GUIDE

MOUNTAINEERING

Mountaineering is a sport that requires special skill, equipment, and endurance.

The most important thing in climbing is safety. Beginning climbers should start out slowly, taking one-day hikes or backpacking trips to strengthen muscles. Practice foot- and handholds by scrambling over boulders, and never attempt a difficult climb without an experienced climber present.

Use of the rope is the most crucial skill for a climber, and many climbers spend months mastering belaying and rappelling. On most climbs, two or three people are roped together. One person is chosen as the leader and covers the route first. The second climber follows, and then the third.

CLIMBING TERMS

Belayer: The person who handles the ropes and protects the climber from a fall.

Bowline: A special knot used to connect the ropes to the climber.

Carabiner: An aluminum clip with a gate that opens and snaps shut, connecting climbing hardware with the rope.

Chimney: Openings in a mountainside wide enough for a climber to get inside.

Commands: Short, easy-to-understand climbing instructions exchanged between the lead man, belayer, and end man.

Ice Ax: A special ax that has a pick on one end and a blade on the other, designed for climbing snow- or ice-covered peaks.

Pitons: Metal spikes with rings on one end that can be hammered into cracks in rock and used as handholds.

Rappelling: Descending a mountain by sliding down a rope that is anchored at the top.

Don't miss all the exciting action!

**Read the other action-packed books in
Gary Paulsen's
WORLD OF ADVENTURE!**

The Legend of Red Horse Cavern

Will Little Bear Tucker and his friend Sarah Thompson have heard the eerie Apache legend many times. Will's grandfather especially loves to tell them about Red Horse—an Indian brave who betrayed his people, was beheaded, and now haunts the Sacramento Mountain range, searching for his head. To Will and Sarah it was just a story—until they decide to explore a newfound mountain cave, a cave filled with dangerous treasures.

Deep underground Will and Sarah uncover an old chest stuffed with a million dollars. But now armed bandits are after them. When they find a gold Apache statue hidden in a skull, it seems Red Horse is hunting them, too. Then they lose their way, and each step they take in the damp dark cavern could be their last.

Rodomonte's Revenge

Friends Brett Wilder and Tom Houston are video game whizzes. So when a new virtual reality arcade called Rodomonte's Revenge opens near their home, they make sure that they are its first customers. The game is awesome. There are flaming fire rivers to jump, beastly buzz-bugs to fight, and ugly tunnel spiders to escape. If they're good enough they'll face

Rodomonte, an evil giant waiting to do battle within his hidden castle.

But soon after they play the game, strange things start happening to Brett and Tom. The computer is taking over their minds. Now everything that happens in the game is happening in real life. A buzzbug could gnaw off their ear. Rodomonte could smash them to bits. Brett and Tom have no choice but to play Rodomonte's Revenge again. This time they'll be playing for their lives.

Escape from Fire Mountain

". . . please anybody . . . fire . . . need help."

That's the urgent cry thirteen-year-old Nikki Roberts hears over the CB radio the weekend she's left alone in her family's hunting lodge. The message also says that the sender is trapped near a bend in the river. Nikki knows it's dangerous, but she has to try to help. She paddles her canoe downriver, coming closer to the thick black smoke of the forest fire with each stroke. When she reaches the bend, Nikki climbs onshore. There, covered with soot and huddled on a rock ledge, sit two small children.

Nikki struggles to get the children to safety. Flames roar around them. Trees splinter to the ground. But as Nikki tries to escape the fire, she doesn't know that two poachers are also hot on her trail. They fear that she and the children have seen too much of their illegal operation—and they'll do anything to keep the kids from making it back to the lodge alive.

Look for these adventures coming soon!

Hook 'Em, Snotty!

Bobbie Walker loves working on her grandfather's ranch. She hates the fact that her cousin Alex is coming up from Los Angeles to visit and will probably ruin her summer. Alex can barely ride a horse and doesn't know the first thing about roping. There is no way Alex can survive a ride into the flats to round up wild cattle. But Bobbie is going to have to let her tag along anyway.

Out in the flats the weather turns bad. Even worse, Bobbie knows that she'll have to watch out for the Bledsoe boys, two mischievous brothers who are usually up to no good. When the boys rustle the girls' cattle, Bobbie and Alex team up to teach the Bledsoes a lesson. But with the wild bull Diablo on the loose, the fun and games may soon turn deadly serious.

Danger on Midnight River

Daniel Martin doesn't want to go to Camp Eagle Nest. He wants to spend the summer as he always does: with his uncle Smitty in the Rocky Mountains. Daniel is a slow learner, but most kids call him retarded. Daniel knows that at camp things are only going to get worse. His nightmare comes true when he and three bullies must ride the camp van together.

On the trip to camp Daniel is the butt of the bullies' jokes. He ignores them and concentrates on the roads outside. He thinks they may be lost. As the van crosses a wooden bridge, the planks suddenly give way. The van plunges into the raging river below. Daniel struggles to shore, but the driver and the other boys are nowhere to be found. It's freezing, and night is setting in. Daniel faces a difficult decision. He could save himself . . . or risk everything to try to rescue the others, too.

The Gorgon Slayer

Eleven-year-old Warren Trumbull has a strange job. He works for Prince Charming's Damsel in Distress Rescue Agency, saving people from hideous monsters, evil warlocks, and wicked witches. Then one day Warren gets the most dangerous assignment of all: He must exterminate a Gorgon.

Gorgons are horrible creatures. They have green scales, clawed fingers, and snakes for hair. They also have the power to turn people to stone. Warren doesn't want to be a stone statue for the rest of his life. He'll need all his courage and skill—and his secret plan—to become a true Gorgon slayer.

The Gorgon howls as Warren enters the dark basement to do battle. Warren lowers his eyes, raises his sword and shield, and leaps into action. But will his plan work?

Cool sleuths, hot on the case!
Read Gary Paulsen's hilarious
Culpepper Adventures.

Coach Amos

Amos and Dunc have their hands full when their
school principal asks *them* to coach a local T-ball
team. For one thing, nobody on the team even
knows first base from left field, and the season
opener is coming right up. And then there's that sin-
ister-looking gangster driving by in his long black
limo and making threats. Can Dunc and Amos fend
off screaming tots, nervous mothers, and the mob,
and be there when the ump yells "Play ball"?

Amos and the Alien

When Amos and his best friend, Dunc, have a close
encounter with an extraterrestrial named Girrk,
Dunc thinks they should report their findings to
NASA. But Amos has other plans. He not only
promises to help Girrk find a way back to his planet,
he invites him to hide out under his bed! Then
weird things start to happen—Scruff can't move,
Amos scores a game-winning *touchdown,* and Dunc
knows Girrk is behind Amos's new powers. What's
the mysterious alien really up to?

Dunc and Amos Meet the Slasher

Why is mild-mannered Amos dressing in leather, slicking back his hair, strutting around the cafeteria, and going by a phony name? Could it be because of that new kid, Slasher, who's promised to eat Amos for lunch? Or has Amos secretly gone undercover? Amos and his pal Dunc have some hot leads and are close to cracking a stolen stereo racket, but Dunc is worried Amos has taken things too far!

Dunc and the Greased Sticks of Doom

Five . . . four . . . three . . . two . . . Olympic superstar Francesco Bartoli is about to hurl himself down the face of a mountain in another attempt to clinch the world slalom speed record. Cheering fans and snapping cameras are everywhere. But someone is out to stop him, and Dunc thinks he knows who it is. Can Dunc get to the gate in time to save the day? Will Amos survive longer than fifteen minutes on the icy slopes?

Amos's Killer Concert Caper

Amos is desperate. He's desperate for two tickets to the romantic event of his young life . . . the Road Kill concert! He'll do anything to get them because he heard from a friend of a friend of a friend of Melissa Hansen that she's way into Road Kill. But when he enlists the help of his best friend, Dunc, he winds up with more than he bargained for . . . backstage, with a mystery to solve.

Amos Gets Married

Everybody knows Amos Binder is crazy in love with Melissa Hansen. Only, Melissa hasn't given any indication that she even knows Amos exists as a lifeform. That is, until now. Suddenly, things with Melissa are different. A wave, a wink—an affectionate "snookems"?! Can this really be Melissa . . . and *Amos*? Dunc is determined to get to the bottom of it all, but who can blame Amos if his feet don't touch the ground?

CULPEPPER ADVENTURES

For laugh-out-loud fun, join Dunc and Amos and take the Culpepper challenge! Gary Paulsen's Culpepper Adventures— Bet you can't read just one!

☐ 0-440-40790-7 DUNC AND AMOS AND THE RED TATTOOS.....$3.25/$3.99 Can.

☐ 0-440-40874-1 DUNC'S UNDERCOVER CHRISTMAS................$3.50/$4.50 Can.

☐ 0-440-40883-0 THE WILD CULPEPPER CRUISE.......................$3.50/$4.50 Can.

☐ 0-440-40893-8 DUNC AND THE HAUNTED CASTLE..................$3.50/$4.50 Can.

☐ 0-440-40902-0 COWPOKES AND DESPERADOES.....................$3.50/$4.50 Can.

☐ 0-440-40928-4 PRINCE AMOS..$3.50/$4.50 Can.

☐ 0-440-40930-6 COACH AMOS...$3.50/$4.50 Can.

☐ 0-440-40990-X AMOS AND THE ALIENS...................................$3.50/$4.50 Can.

Bantam Doubleday Dell Books for Young Readers
2451 South Wolf Road
Des Plaines, IL 60018

Please send the items I have checked above. I'm enclosing $_____ (please add $2.50 to cover postage and handling). Send check or money order, no cash or C.O.D.s please.

_____
Name

_____
Address

_____
City   State   Zip

Please allow four to six weeks for delivery.
Prices and availability subject to change without notice.   **BFYR 29 6/94**